Rancid headed for the door. "You've got your assignment. I expect a full report in my office by tonight!" Rancid slammed the door as he left.

Cat was beaming. "We're going to find that french fry, Dog, I can feel it in our bones!"

But Dog was still upset. "Cat, do we have to spy on our friends?"

"Dog, we can't let our morals stand in the way of truth, justice, and the chance to get one million dollars!" exclaimed Cat. "If they're innocent, then they have nothing to worry about. Trust me. When have I ever steered you wrong?"

CatDog Undercover

by Steven Banks
illustrated by David Maxey

Simon Spotlight / Nickelodeon

Based on the TV series *CatDog*®
created by Peter Hannan as seen on Nickelodeon®

Editorial Consultants: Peter Hannan and Robert Lamoreaux
Additional assistance provided by the CatDog Production Team.

SIMON SPOTLIGHT
An imprint of Simon & Schuster Children's Publishing Division
1230 Avenue of the Americas, New York, New York 10020

Produced by Bumpy Slide Books
Manufactured in the United States of America

First Edition   2 4 6 8 10 9 7 5 3 1

ISBN 0-689-83009-2

Library of Congress Catalog Card Number 99-75605

CatDog was walking out of the Nearburg Movie Theater. They had just seen *Mean Bob Meets Evil Eric Part 6: The Really Good Sequel That's Much Better Than Part 5, We Promise*.

Suddenly they heard a boy selling newspapers. "Extra! Extra!" he yelled. "Read all about it! Robbery at The Nearburg Hall of Cool Neat Stuff!"

CatDog immediately bought a paper.

"Someone stole the World's Longest French Fry!" exclaimed Dog.

"That's awful, that's horrible, that's downright un-Nearburgian!" added Cat.

The Nearburg Hall of Cool Neat Stuff had the coolest and neatest collection of stuff

in Nearburg. They had a potato that looked like a bicycle, a bicycle that looked like a potato, the entire history of Nearburg written in Chinese on the head of a pin, a pirate ship made out of used toothpicks, the world's oldest piece of black licorice, and the world's biggest ball of belly button lint.

But as everyone in Nearburg knew, the coolest and neatest item in the whole collection was the World's Longest French Fry. Every year on March 30, the anniversary of its discovery, everybody in Nearburg celebrated at the French Fry Festival. They sang french fry songs, played french fry games, and dressed up as french fries and jumped into a swimming pool filled with ketchup. And now someone had stolen their most beloved and amazing artifact!

"Who would want to steal that?" Cat wondered out loud.

"Someone who likes to steal things?" suggested Dog.

"That's a good guess," replied Cat.

"Gee, Cat," said Dog, "this sounds like the beginning of an exciting adventure filled with intrigue, danger, and a few laughs!"

"Why do you say that?" asked Cat.

Dog shrugged his shoulders. "I don't know. I just have a hunch."

The next morning, CatDog was watching television. Dog was gnawing on a crispy bone and Cat was eating the last piece of homemade catfish pie.

Mrs. Littlebottom, the third richest person in town and the owner of The Nearburg Hall of Cool Neat Stuff, was appearing on the *Nearburg Morning News*. She was very upset. A tear ran down her cheek as she spoke.

"I am heartbroken that someone would

steal the World's Longest French Fry!" she cried. "As you know, it was discovered twenty-seven years ago by my son, Dinky Littlebottom, at Greasy Greaseburgers. And now some thief has stolen our most precious possession, the pride of Nearburg! I call upon Mayor Rancid Rabbit to hire a special detective and launch a complete investigation! In addition, I will be offering a reward of one million dollars for the safe return of my precious french fry!"

Cat sat up on the sofa. His eyes lit up. "One million dollars! Dog, we *have* to find that french fry!"

Just then there was a knock at CatDog's door. It was Mayor Rancid Rabbit.

"Hi, Mr. Mayor," said Dog. "Come on in."

"Listen, boys. I need your help," said Rancid, sitting down on the sofa. "I want to hire you two to be my special detectives and investigate this missing french fry case."

"We get to be detectives?" asked Dog excitedly. "Hi-ho—"

"Wait a minute, Dog!" Cat interrupted. He turned to Rancid. "That's the police's job."

Rancid nodded his head. "Normally, yes. But I took them all off the case. I need someone special. I'll pay you a hundred dollars a day, plus expenses for your services."

Cat's eyes lit up again. "A hundred dollars!"

"Yes," said Rancid. "I need someone who has a great hunting ability and a great sense of smell, but someone who can also sneak around quietly."

"That's us!" proclaimed Dog. "Cat can sneak around without making a sound."

"Yes, I've heard he's a real sneak," Rancid replied.

"And I'm a good hunter and smeller!" added Dog. "I can smell dirty socks from two miles away. Three miles if there's a wind!" Dog stuck his nose out the window and sniffed. "I can smell Mr. Sunshine's socks right now! He's over at the bowling alley on Fifth Street!"

"Perfect!" said Rancid, standing up. "So, will you accept the job?"

"You betcha!" shouted Dog. "Hi-ho—"

"Wait a minute!" Cat interrupted again. "What about the reward?" he asked.

"Reward?" asked Rancid. "What reward?"

"Mrs. Littlebottom's offering one million dollars," said Cat. "Can we keep the reward if we find the french fry?"

Rancid knew he had to think fast. "Why of course you can! I don't care about money. All I want is the criminal behind bars!" he said.

Cat was delighted. They would be paid for working as detectives *and* they'd get the reward if they found the french fry! What could be better?

Cat shook Rancid's hand. "Mr. Mayor, you've got yourself a pair of detectives!"

"Now can I say 'hi-ho-diggety,' Cat?" asked Dog.

"Yes," Cat answered.

"Hi-ho-diggety! We get to be detectives!" cried Dog.

Rancid pulled out an important looking piece of paper. "Here's a list of the top six suspects who may have committed the crime."

Rancid handed CatDog the paper. When CatDog saw the names, they were both puzzled.

Cat read the names out loud. "KEIRHS? FFILC? EBUL? SIVREM? PALGNUD? WOLSNIW? Who are these people?" he asked.

"I've never heard of any of them," added a confused Dog.

Rancid rolled his eyes. "That's 'cause you're reading the list upside down, you dopes!"

CatDog turned the paper right side up.

They couldn't believe what they saw. The names on the list were Shriek, Cliff, Lube, Mervis, Dunglap, and Winslow!

"You think that one of them took the french fry?" asked Cat.

"Mervis and Dunglap wouldn't steal anything," Dog said.

"Oh, yeah?" said Rancid, raising his eyebrows. "They do volunteer work at The Nearburg Hall of Cool Neat Stuff. They could have stolen the french fry as easy as pie! Speaking of pie, do you have any? I'm starving."

Cat shook his head. "Sorry, I just ate the last piece."

"What about Winslow?" asked Dog. "Why is he on the list?"

"Because he's a rat!" said Rancid. "Never trust a rat. Especially a blue one."

"But Winslow's our friend!" Dog declared.

"That rotten rodent is *your* friend," Cat replied. "Not mine."

Rancid put his arm around Dog. "Don't think of him as a friend, think of him as a suspect. Every great detective knows that you can leave no stone unturned and no friend unsuspected! Trust no one, suspect everyone!"

"But I don't think Winslow would steal anything," said Dog.

Rancid smiled. "Hah! I used to say the same thing about my mother!"

"What did she steal?" asked Dog.

"Nothing, yet," said Rancid. "But I've got a man watching her twenty-four hours a day, just in case."

Rancid headed for the door. "You've got your assignment. I expect a full report in my office by tonight! And next time, save me some pie!" Rancid slammed the door as he left.

Cat was beaming. "We're going to find that french fry, Dog, I can feel it in our bones!"

But Dog was still upset. "Cat, do we have to spy on our friends?"

"It might not be one of our friends," said Cat. "It might be one of the Greasers."

"But why would one of the Greasers steal a french fry?" Dog wondered.

"Dog, we can't let our morals stand in the way of truth, justice, and the chance to get one million dollars!" exclaimed Cat. "If they're innocent, then they have nothing to worry about. Trust me. When have I ever steered you wrong?"

Dog pulled out a little notebook and opened it. "It says here about 127 times."

Cat tossed the notebook aside. "Forget all those other times. *This* is different!"

"Okay, Cat," Dog finally agreed. "Let's start spying! I can use my official Mean Bob Super Detective Spy Kit!"

Dog had sent in 1,000 box tops from Sugar Bomb cereal and waited two years to get his official Mean Bob Super Detective Spy Kit. It had a special periscope for secretly spying on people. It also had a stethoscope like doctors use to listen to your heart, but this one was for listening through walls and windows. There was a magnifying glass, a whistle, two disguises, and a decoder ring. Batteries were not included.

"Let the spying begin!" announced Dog. "Who's our first suspect, Cat?"

Chapter Two

Just then Winslow popped out of his hole. "Hiya, CatDog!" he said. "What's new with you two?"

Dog started to say something, but Cat clamped his paw over Dog's mouth.

Winslow went over to the refrigerator, opened it, and took out an ice-cold can of extrafoamy root beer. "Hey, I heard somebody stole that oversized piece of french fried potato from The Nearburg Hall of Cool Neat Stuff."

Cat leaned in close to Winslow. "Oh, really? Well, who do you think would do something like that?" he asked.

Winslow opened his root beer and took a sip. "How the heck should I know?" he

replied. "I ain't no detective! See ya later. I got important work to do!" And with that, Winslow disappeared back into his hole.

"That was very suspicious!" said Cat. "Write that down!"

"Okeydokey, Cat!" said Dog as opened up his notebook. "What am I writing down?"

Cat began: "First: Winslow knew about the french fry. Second: He said he had 'important work to do.' And third: I've never trusted that little rat from the day I met him!"

CatDog set up their equipment outside Winslow's hole in the wall. They decided to use Dog's official Mean Bob Super Periscope. It was like a periscope on a submarine except you could twist and turn it. Cat carefully put it in Winslow's hole and looked through the eyepiece.

"Do you see anything suspicious, Cat?" whispered Dog.

"Not yet," answered Cat. "But I'll tell you one thing, Winslow has a very nice collection of postmodern art."

Cat kept looking, twisting and turning the periscope through Winslow's home. He saw Winslow's library, his private movie theater, his indoor swimming pool, and his big-screen TV.

"Do you see the french fry, Cat?" asked an impatient Dog.

Cat shook his head. "No, I don't even see Win—wait a minute, there's that little stinker!"

"What's he doing?" asked Dog excitedly.

Cat peered through the periscope. "He's sitting at his desk . . . he's opening a drawer . . . he's taking out a piece of paper . . . he's picking up a pen . . . he's writing a letter!"

"That's all? See, I knew he didn't steal that french fry!" Dog exclaimed happily.

"Oh, really?" said Cat. "That could be a ransom letter he's writing. Asking for money for the safe return of the french fry. Reel in the periscope, Dog. I've seen enough."

"Why don't we just *ask* Winslow what he's writing?" Dog suggested.

Cat looked at Dog, shocked. "Ask him? Don't be ridiculous! No true detective *talks* to his suspects. Move Winslow's name to the top of our list of most suspicious characters!"

Dog had to convince Cat he was wrong, so he stuck his nose in Winslow's hole in the wall and took a big sniff. "Cat, I don't smell any french fry in there."

"Winslow could have it hidden in an airtight compartment," said Cat. "Now, let's go! We still have to check out our next two suspects: Mervis and Dunglap."

Chapter Three

Mervis and Dunglap lived next door to each other on the twelfth floor of an apartment building. CatDog camped out in front of their building so they could figure out their next move.

Dog tapped Cat on the shoulder. "How are we gonna spy on Mervis and Dunglap without them seeing us spying on them?"

Cat pointed at a window washer who was cleaning the windows on one side of the building. "A super detective like myself always figures out a way! When that window washer takes his lunch break, we'll sneak up onto his platform and spy in Mervis's and Dunglap's windows."

"That's brilliant, Cat!" said Dog proudly.

"Of course it's brilliant. *I* thought of it," boasted Cat.

At 12:02 P.M. the window washer lowered his platform to the ground, picked up his lunch pail, and went to lunch. CatDog carefully climbed onto the window washer's platform. They pulled themselves up to the bottom edge of Mervis's window and peeked in through the glass.

"Cat, it's so weird. Do you really think Mervis and Dunglap could be the robbers?" asked Dog.

"Those two do a lot of weird things," said Cat. "They play Ping-Pong on their roof in their pajamas, they eat Mexican food with chopsticks, and they roller-skate underwater. I wouldn't put it past them to steal the World's Longest French Fry."

CatDog was in luck. Dunglap was visiting

Mervis. The window was closed, so Cat used Dog's Mean Bob Super Detective Stethoscope to stick on the window so he could hear what Mervis and Dunglap were saying. As usual, Mervis and Dunglap were arguing.

"I want to put it in my apartment!" said Dunglap.

"No, way! We are putting it in my apartment, in the closet!" said Mervis, stomping his feet.

"My closet's better!" yelled Dunglap.

"My closet's bigger!" countered Mervis. He then walked over to his closet, opened the door, and stepped inside: "See?"

"No, it isn't," said Dunglap as he closed the closet door. It banged into Mervis's head.

"Ow! My head!" cried Mervis from inside the closet. "You did that on purpose!"

"No, I didn't," said Dunglap. "Your big head got in the way!"

"My head's not big!" yelled Mervis.

"It is too! Now come out of the closet so we can put it in *my* closet!" Dunglap yelled back.

"Not until you apologize!" cried Mervis.

Outside the window, Dog whispered to Cat, "I don't *see* any french fry and I don't *smell* any french fry. I *knew* they were innocent."

"Dog, Dog, Dog. Don't you see?" asked Cat. "They're deciding where to *hide* the french fry. And a closet is the perfect place!"

"Why don't we just knock on the window and ask Mervis and Dunglap what they're doing?" Dog suggested.

"Detectives don't ask questions, they spy and snoop!" replied Cat. "Besides, I think we've found our thieves."

Dog was confused. "But you said before that Winslow stole it."

Cat grabbed the rope and started to

lower them down to the ground. "You can never have too many suspects. Now, come on, we have one more stop to make: the Greasers' house."

Chapter Four

CatDog had to be extracareful when spying on the Greasers. If the Greasers saw them, CatDog knew they would be chased and pounded. So this time, they put on the official Mean Bob Super Detective Spy Disguises. Cat wore a big, black mustache, a monocle, and a top hat. Dog wore eyeglasses, a blond wig, and a lady's sweater.

As they walked down a busy street in Nearburg, Cat was feeling rather confident about their plan. "No one will recognize us in our brilliant disguises!" he boasted to Dog.

"Hey there, CatDog!" came a voice from across the street.

CatDog turned to see Randolph Grant,

the handsome and dashing man-about-town, waving at them. "Your new look is wild and wonderful and I *love* it!" he called. "What a fabulous fiesta of fashion fun!"

"Hi, Randolph!" yelled Dog, waving back. "We got it from my official Mean Bob Super Detective Spy Kit!"

Cat grabbed Dog and pulled him behind a mailbox. "Dog, what are you doing?! We're supposed to be in disguise! No one is supposed to know who we are!"

"Sorry, Cat," whispered Dog. Then Dog poked his head out from behind the mailbox and yelled across the street, "Hey, Randolph! We're not who you think we are! We're somebody else! We're not CatDog!"

Cat rolled his eyes. "Just forget it, Sherlock. C'mon!" he said as they tore off their disguises and scrambled away.

The Greasers lived in a beat-up house,

on a crummy block, on the wrong side of the tracks, in the roughest part of Nearburg. It was a tough neighborhood and the Greasers were the toughest dogs there.

CatDog was nervous as they tiptoed up to their enemies' house. But they were detectives—and they had a job to do!

Dog started to get more nervous. "I wouldn't accuse the Greasers for a million bucks!" he declared.

"We *are* doing this for a million bucks, remember?!" Cat replied.

"Oh, yeah," Dog said and shrugged.

Then CatDog crept up to the Greasers' window and tried to peek in. They couldn't see a thing. The window was filthy. It looked like it hadn't been cleaned for twenty years. Actually it hadn't been cleaned in twenty-one years, but who's counting?

Dog wiped the glass off with his paw

because Cat didn't want to get his paws dirty. They peered inside. Cliff was exercising, lifting their sofa up and down over his head. His face was bright red as he huffed and puffed, "Ninety-seven . . . sixty-two . . . twelve!"

Sitting on the sofa was Lube, trying to tie his shoe. He was holding up the shoelace and saying, "The rabbit . . . goes in the little hole and—"

Suddenly, the door banged open and Shriek walked in carrying a big, black book. "Okay, boys! Time to get to work," she announced.

Cliff put down the sofa and Lube put down his shoe.

Outside the window, Cat wrote in his notebook, "Shriek is carrying a big, black, mysterious book. Very suspicious!"

Shriek opened the book, cleared her throat, and began to read aloud, "*Bonjour.*"

"*Bonjour*," Cliff repeated.

Lube said nothing. Cliff poked him in the ribs. "Lube, you're suppose to say what Shriek says!"

"Duh . . . okay . . . What did she say?" asked Lube.

Shriek put her paws on her hips and yelled, "I said '*bonjour*' you bonehead!"

Lube repeated, "I said *bonjour*, you bonehead."

"Close enough!" said Shriek. "Let's continue!"

"They're all speaking French," Cat whispered to Dog. "If *that* doesn't connect them to the crime, I don't know what does! Come on, let's go!"

CatDog dropped down from the window and snuck away from the Greasers' house.

Dog was confused. "I don't get it, Cat. So, *now* you think the Greasers stole the french fry?"

Cat was getting frustrated. "It's so obvious, Dog. The Greasers were speaking French. What do French people eat?"

"French bread," said Dog.

"What else?" asked Cat.

"French toast," said Dog.

"What else?!" asked Cat, getting more impatient.

Dog kept guessing. "Omelettes? Soufflés? Snails? Truffles?"

"WHAT ELSE?!" yelled Cat.

"Can you give me a hint?" asked Dog.

"French fries!" screamed Cat.

"Is that a hint?" asked Dog.

"No! It's the answer!" said Cat.

"Then we better go tell Rancid, quick!" said Dog.

Cat shook his head. "How did I ever get attached to him?!"

Chapter Five

Rancid Rabbit was sitting in his big chair, at his big desk, in his big office, with big windows, looking over the big city. Behind him was a big painting of his great-grandfather, Rotten Rabbit, the first mayor of Nearburg.

CatDog sat across from Rancid and told him everything they had heard and seen. They told him about Winslow and the mysterious letter, Mervis and Dunglap and the closet, and the Greasers speaking French.

"Nice work, boys!" Rancid said. "I knew you'd be great detectives!"

"Thank you, Mr. Mayor," said Cat. "When do we get the reward?"

"When you find the french fry.

Tomorrow morning I'll get you a search warrant and you can search all the suspects' houses," replied Rancid.

"Which one of them do you think did it, Mr. Mayor?" asked Dog.

Rancid stood up. "I'm not sure," he began, "but, just to be safe, I'm going to throw them all in jail!"

"All of them?" asked Dog.

"Better to be safe than sorry," Rancid replied.

And with that, Rancid arrested Cliff, Lube, Shriek, Mervis, Dunglap, and Winslow, and threw them all in the Nearburg County Jail.

"I want my lawyer!" Winslow yelled.

"I want my mommy!" Mervis yelled.

"I want my own cell with a queen-sized bed, a view of the ocean, and a complimentary terry cloth robe!" Dunglap yelled.

"Duh . . . I want to learn how to tie my shoe," said Lube.

"This is Greaser harassment!" shrieked Shriek.

"What are we doin' in here, anyway?" demanded Cliff.

Rancid stood outside the jail cell. "Quiet down, hooligans!" he demanded. "One of you stole the World's Longest French Fry! And I'm going to keep all of you in here until one of you confesses!" Then Rancid put the key to the cell in his pocket.

"I didn't steal that freaky french fry!" said Winslow. "I hate french fries. I'm an onion ring kind of rat."

"It wasn't me," Dunglap called to Rancid. "I'm on a french-fry-free diet!"

Mervis poked his head through the bars of the cell. "I haven't had a french fry for ten years, ever since I accidentally poked myself in the eye with one," he confessed. "Boy, did that hurt!"

Dunglap shook his head in disgust. "Mervis, you big baby, that didn't hurt!"

"Yes, it did!" yelled Mervis, and like always, they started to fight.

Shriek pushed Mervis and Dunglap aside. "I'm allergic to french fries! I break out in spots! If I eat one of those things, I loc   like a leopard!" she yelled at Rancid throug   the bars.

"I don't go for no foreign food!'   Cliff bellowed.

Lube scratched his head. "Duh . . . I wouldn't eat a fly . . . even if it was French."

Rancid nodded. "Just as I thought, everybody's claiming innocence!" he said. "Well, according to the detectives I hired, who spied on you, *all* of you were engaged in suspicious activities!"

"What detectives?" yelled Cliff.

"What suspicious activities?" cried Shriek.

"Who spied on us?" demanded Mervis.

"It was none other than your old friends CatDog!" said Rancid with a grin as he walked out the door.

Meanwhile, CatDog was safe at home, sitting on their sofa. Cat was enjoying a cold glass of clam juice, feeling very pleased with himself. "Dog, my friend, we are a great pair of detectives! Tomorrow we'll find that french fry, get that reward, and then it's party time! Just think what we can do with a million dollars! I'm going to buy a dozen jet skis!"

Cat gazed over at Dog, who didn't look so excited. "Hey? What's the matter with you?"

"I still don't think anyone we spied on stole that french fry," said Dog.

Cat sipped his drink and sighed. "Dog,

you saw the evidence. One of them had to have done it!"

"I don't care!" said Dog, getting up. "I don't think they did it and I'm gonna prove it! A true detective leaves no stone unturned!"

With that, Dog started for the door, dragging Cat off the sofa and spilling his clam juice.

"Hey! Where are you going?" demanded Cat.

"I'm going down to that jail to talk to them like we should have in the first place!" replied Dog. He opened the door. "Are you coming with me?"

Cat sighed. "Do I have a choice?"

Chapter Six

When CatDog got to the jail, they faced a very angry group of prisoners.

Cliff shook his fist at them and bellowed, "When we get outta here, we're gonna make you sorry you wuz ever born!"

"Dog! How could you?" cried Shriek. "I thought we had a mutual understanding!"

Lube said nothing. He was still trying to tie his shoe.

Mervis looked at Dog. "I thought you were our friends, CatDog!"

"With friends like you, who needs enemies?" added Dunglap. "You're nothing but low-down, dirty rats!"

"Hey!" exclaimed Winslow. "As a rat, I

resent that remark!" Then Winslow turned to Dog and said, "I can believe that Cat would do something as low-down as this, but you? Spying on me? Dog, you broke my heart!"

Dog started to speak, but Cat interrupted him.

"Wait a minute! We found evidence," Cat explained. "You were all doing very suspicious things!"

Cat pointed at Winslow. "We saw you writing a letter," Cat said. "It looked like a ransom note, asking for money for the safe return of the french fry!"

Winslow reached into his pocket. He pulled out the same piece of paper that CatDog saw him writing on and handed it to Dog. "This is what I was writing, Mr. Jump To Conclusions!" he explained.

Dog read the letter out loud, "Dear Mom, How are things in Florida? Thanks for the cheese and crackers, they were delicious. Love your favorite son, Winslow T. Oddfellow."

Dog was embarrassed. "I'm sorry, Winslow."

Cat smiled weakly. "No hard feelings, Winslow?"

"There are plenty of hard feelings!" Winslow cried, shaking his tiny fist. "And when I get outta here, I'm gonna give you some hard feelings right on your skulls!"

Cat turned to the others. "Okay, so Winslow is innocent. But Mervis and Dunglap, we saw you arguing about hiding something in the closet!"

Mervis and Dunglap looked at each other and blushed.

"See! They're blushing!" Cat pointed out. "What were you going to put in the closet?"

Mervis looked down at the floor. "We can't tell you."

"Ah ha!" said Cat. "It's the french fry! I knew it! Guilty! Case closed!"

Dunglap turned to Mervis: "We better tell 'em, Mervy."

"It was a birthday gift for you," Mervis explained. "We were trying to figure out where to hide it."

Dog gulped. "A . . . birthday gift for us?"

"It was a jet ski," Dunglap confessed.

Tears came to Cat's eyes, his lower lip trembled. "A jet ski? For us? All my life I've wanted a jet ski!"

"Well, you ain't getting it now, you rats!" Dunglap yelled.

"Hey!" Winslow shouted. "How many times do I have to tell you to stop calling them rats, you weasel!"

Cat laughed nervously. "Okay, everyone makes a little, teensy, tiny mistake once in a while."

"*Tiny mistake?!*" cried Mervis. "You got us put in jail!"

"Why didn't you just *ask* us what we were doing?" Dunglap asked.

Dog glared at Cat. "That's what *I* wanted to do, but *someone* wouldn't let me!"

"Okay, okay," Cat said. "But if Winslow, Mervis, and Dunglap are all innocent, then it has to be the Greasers. We caught them all speaking French! As in *french* fry. Coincidence? I think not!"

"*Au contraire!* What if we *were* speaking French? So what?" demanded Shriek.

"Ah ha! You admit it!" Cat cried.

"Dat's cuz Shriek was teaching us how to speak French," said Cliff.

Shriek pushed her nose through the bars of the cell. "We're going to the International Pounding Convention in Paris this year and we want to know how to speak the language."

Cliff glared at CatDog, "And when we learn those new pounding techniques, we're gonna give you a personal demonstration!"

Lube didn't say anything. He had just tied his ear to his shoe.

Dog looked up. "Mervis, Dunglap, Winslow, Cliff, Lube, Shriek—we're sorry," he pleaded. "Can you forgive us?"

"NO!" they all yelled from the cell.

"Some friends you turned out to be," said Dunglap.

"And some detectives!" added Winslow. "You couldn't even find out who stole that overgrown french fry!"

"I did it!" announced Lube.

Everyone froze. They all turned to Lube, sitting in the corner.

"You stole that french fry, Lube?" asked a shocked Cliff.

Lube smiled proudly. "No. I tied my shoe!"

After a polite round of applause, Winslow banged on the bars. "Okay, CatDog, world's worst detectives, unlock this door and let us out of here!"

Cat cleared his throat nervously and said, "Uh, we can't. Rancid has the key."

"Then go get it!" barked Cliff.

CatDog ran to the door.

"We'll be right back!" called Dog over his shoulder. "Don't go anywhere!"

CatDog jumped on their bike and headed off to Rancid's office. Dog was pedaling as fast as he could while Cat steered.

"Hi-ho-diggety! I knew they were innocent!" cried Dog.

"You were right, Dog," admitted Cat. "But we still haven't solved the case. Who stole the french fry?"

Chapter Seven

Rancid Rabbit was in his office, looking up at the big painting of his great-grandfather, Rotten Rabbit, hanging on the wall above his desk. "Well, Great-Grand Pappy, are you proud of me?" he asked as he moved the painting. Behind it was a safe. He turned the dial and opened it. Then he put on a pair of gloves, so as not to leave paw prints, and he pulled out the World's Longest French Fry! Rancid was the thief!

"Hee, hee, hee," Rancid laughed. "I've pulled off the heist of the century! No one would ever suspect that a public official would do anything bad. And hiring CatDog to be detectives kept everyone out of my way. I knew

those goofballs could never discover who really stole it. And I knew old Mrs. Littlebottom would offer a big reward! Now I can pretend to find it myself, return it, and get the million dollar reward!" He looked at his reflection in a mirror. "Rancid, you are one bad bunny!"

"You sure are!" came a voice from the doorway.

Rancid quickly turned around in horror to see CatDog! They had been there for the past five minutes and had heard *everything*.

"Darn!" said Rancid. "I hate it when people walk in while I'm describing my crimes out loud!"

"Say cheeseburger!" called Dog as he took a picture of Rancid holding the World's Longest French Fry. Dog held up the camera and proudly declared, "Now that's what I call evidence!"

"If the french fry fits, you must convict!" added Cat.

Rancid looked around the room. He had to think fast. "Well, I guess you got me fair and square, CatDog. I give up. I know when I'm beat."

"That's right!" said Cat. "So now we'll just call the police and then we'll take that big french fry and go collect our big, fat reward!"

Rancid gave a sly smile. "May I ask one little favor? Could I shake the hands of the two brilliant detectives who solved the crime?"

Rancid held his paw out to CatDog.

"Well, I guess that would be all right," said Cat as he reached out to shake Rancid's hand.

But suddenly, Rancid grabbed the camera and smashed it to the floor! Then he pulled out the film and tore it up!

"He ruined the film!" Dog yelled. "Now we'll never prove he's the culprit!"

Rancid ran to the door and opened it.

"That is correct, CatDog!" he said. "Now I hate to run, but I have to turn this french fry in and collect my big, fat million dollar reward! Gee, I guess crime *does* pay!" Rancid laughed as he closed the door and locked CatDog in from the other side.

CatDog tried to get out, but it was no use.

"I guess we're not very good detectives, after all," said Dog.

"We should have been spying on Rancid," Cat agreed.

"But, Cat, we saw Rancid with the french fry! Can't we tell somebody?" asked Dog.

"Forget it. No one will believe us," replied Cat.

"Well, on a completely different subject," began Dog, "how are we gonna get out of here?"

"How about screaming at the top of our lungs?" suggested Cat.

"Okay," said Dog.

"HELP!" screamed CatDog.

Three-and-a-half hours later, the janitor let them out.

Chapter Eight

The next day, CatDog went to the ceremony for the return of the World's Longest French Fry at The Nearburg Hall of Cool Neat Stuff. There was a big brass band playing music. There were even balloons and confetti. Rancid rode in a car down Nearburg Avenue while people cheered him as their hero.

CatDog wanted to tell everyone that Rancid was a crook, but they couldn't figure out a way to prove it. They had stayed up all night trying to think of a plan, but they couldn't.

On the platform, the World's Longest French Fry was in a special glass case and there was a big guard standing next to it.

Cat made a face. "I don't want to hear the words 'french fry' again as long as I live," he complained.

"French fries! French fries! French fries! Come and get your french fries!" called Mr. Sunshine as he pushed his french fry cart past CatDog. "Hot and greasy, just the way you like 'em."

Dog was starving as usual. He bought a bag and started eating. "Want a french fry, Cat?" he offered.

Cat glared at Dog. "No, thank you."

On the platform, Mrs. Littlebottom was about to give Rancid his check for one million dollars. "And for finding the World's Longest French Fry and returning it to its rightful home, I would like to present Nearburg's newest hero, Rancid Rabbit, with his well-deserved reward—"

"Hey, Cat! Look!" Dog whispered.

"Don't bother me right now, I'm miserable," said Cat.

"You gotta look at this!" Dog insisted.

"I don't want to look at anything right now!" said Cat, getting angrier.

"But you gotta look at what I found!" begged Dog.

"Okay, what is it?" said Cat, finally turning toward Dog.

Mrs. Littlebottom was just about to hand the million dollar check to Rancid.

"Wait a minute!" yelled a voice from the crowd.

Everyone fell silent.

"Who said that?" Mrs. Littlebottom asked.

Rancid reached out for the check. "It's probably just some troublemaker! Give me the money!" he demanded as he grabbed the check from Mrs. Littlebottom.

"Wait a minute!" yelled the voice again from the crowd. It was Dog! "Look what I have!" Dog yelled.

Dog then proceeded to hold up the longest french fry anyone had ever seen! It was even longer than the World's Longest French Fry that was in the glass case. A *lot* longer! Twice as long, in fact!

Mrs. Littlebottom snatched the check back from Rancid's greedy little paws and tore it up.

"Hey! What are you doing? That's my reward!" yelled Rancid.

"Excuse me, the reward was for the return of the World's Longest French Fry," said Mrs. Littlebottom as she pointed to the french fry onstage. "But *this* is no longer the world's longest french fry!" Then she pointed at Dog. "That dog is holding the World's Longest French Fry."

"But that's not fair!" complained Rancid, stamping his feet.

"I guess crime doesn't pay!" yelled Cat.

The guard took the World's Second Longest French Fry out of the special case. "What shall we do with this one, madam?" he asked.

Mrs. Littlebottom stuck her nose in the air. "I don't care what you do with it. It's worthless now!" she answered.

The guard took a bite out of it. "Needs ketchup," he said.

Rancid was furious. "Wait a minute! I found it and returned it! I want my money!" But nobody was listening to him. Everyone was gathered around Dog, admiring the *new* World's Longest French Fry.

Dog immediately donated his french fry to The Nearburg Hall of Cool Neat Stuff. As CatDog was getting their picture taken by photographers, Dog turned to Cat and said, "Isn't this great? I wish our friends were here to see this."

Suddenly a look of horror came over CatDog's faces. Oops! They had forgotten about their friends and enemies who were still locked in jail! They had never gotten the key from Rancid and gone back to let them out like they had promised.

Just then, in the distance, CatDog saw a group of dogs, a pig, a weasel, and one small rat running toward them. As the group got closer, CatDog could see that it was a very angry group. And when they got even closer, CatDog saw that it was Cliff, Lube, Shriek, Mervis, Dunglap, and Winslow!

"Gee, how do you think they got out of jail?" wondered Dog aloud.

Cat gulped. "I don't know, but I'm not sticking around to find out!" he answered.

"But, Cat, don't you want to see if you can still get our reward?" yelled Dog.

"Come on, I'll give you a reward—I'll buy you a hamburger!" Cat screamed as he started to run.

"Can I get some fries with that?" Dog asked, licking his lips.